This book belongs to

PUFFIN BOOKS

UK | USA | Canada | Ireland | Australia
India | New Zealand | South Africa

Puffin Books is part of the Penguin Random House group of companies
whose addresses can be found at global.penguinrandomhouse.com.

puffinbooks.com

First published 2016
001

Text by Lauren Holowaty

Printed in China

A CIP catalogue record for this book is available from the British Library

ISBN: 978–0–141–36426–1

HAPPY BIRTHDAY Peter!

PUFFIN

It was a special day, and Peter Rabbit's family and friends were planning a VERY special birthday party.

"I'll bring the cake," said Mrs Rabbit. "Lily, please could you get the decorations? And, Benjamin, you're in charge of getting Peter to the party on time."

"You can count on me,"
replied Benjamin proudly.
"What a great day for a sur– "

"SSHHH!"
whispered Peter's little sister,
Cotton-tail, hearing someone
coming towards the burrow.

"A great day for what?"

asked Peter, marching inside.

"Oh, hi, Peter," mumbled Benjamin. "A great day for a . . . erm, a . . ."

"A walk," said Lily. "It's a great day for a walk in the woods."

"Yes, I'll come with you. See you later, Peter," added Benjamin, hurrying out of the burrow.

"Oh, OK," sighed Peter, disappointed. Had they forgotten it was his birthday?

Peter didn't want to go for a walk. He wanted to go on an

extra-special adventure!

"Phew, that was close!"

puffed Lily, when they were far enough away from the burrow. "Peter nearly found out about his own surprise party."

"I know," gasped Benjamin, relieved he hadn't ruined all the plans.

"Now I'll go to get the decorations," said Lily. "You get the balloons, and we'll meet back here after lunch to collect Peter for the party. Let's hop to it!"

When they were out of sight, Mr Tod sneaked out of the bushes. He had heard everything they'd said.

"A surprise party after lunch, you say? Oh, how I love surprises," he sneered.

"I have the perfect one in mind . . . Three little rabbits will make one special

AFTERNOON TEA FOR ME!"

Mr Tod returned home and began planning his very own sneaky surprise.

"I need a foolproof trap,"

he thought. "Hmmm, I could use my fishing rod . . .

. . . No, that won't work . . .

. . . Perhaps some mouth-watering radishes to tempt them?

Hmmm . . . NO."

Just then, something in the corner of the room caught his eye.

"EXCELLENT,"

he said. "I know just how to catch these pesky rabbits."

After lunch, Benjamin and Lily went back to the burrow to collect Peter.

"Hi, Peter!" Benjamin said. "Sorry about earlier – we had to . . . er . . . erm . . ."

"Go and collect something!" Lily added.

Peter thought they were both acting very strangely.

The three friends headed off into the woods.

"Where are we going?" asked Peter curiously. "Can we go to Mr McGregor's garden?"

"Not today," said Lily, bounding ahead. "We're going on a nature walk!"

"Well, how about we go and visit Squirrel Nutkin?" Peter suggested.

"No," said Benjamin, looking closely at a ladybird.

"So where are we going?" Peter replied crossly.

"This way," called Lily, moving a rope off the path.

"**RATS!**" whispered Mr Tod under his breath, as he watched the bunnies walk off.

The first part of his plan had been foiled. But the fiendish fox had more tricks up his sleeve . . .

As the rabbits continued their walk through the woods, Peter began to get a little bored.

"Let's look for tunnels,"

he said, picking up a sack and peering down into a deep, dark hole.

"Be careful, Peter. Hmm, that looks suspiciously like one of Mr Tod's traps," said Lily.

"Come on – we're going to be late," called Benjamin.

"Late for what?" asked Peter.

"**NOTHING!**" Benjamin blushed, hurrying away.

"**You rascally rabbits!**" shouted the fox, coming out of the shadows.

"Now you've ruined my second trap, too. Still, there's more where that came from."

The friends had almost reached the party when Benjamin tripped over a branch.

"Look out!"

shouted Peter. "That looks like another one of Mr Tod's . . ."

yelled the fearsome fox.

It was too late! Benjamin's trip had triggered a cage made of thorny brambles and it came crashing down on top of them.

"Now we'll never make it on time," Lily sighed.
"This is bad, this is really bad," squeaked Benjamin nervously.

Mr Tod sang merrily to himself as he prepared the fire.

"Steam and simmer, bake or stew . . ."

Peter tried yanking on the cage. "It won't budge."

Lily tried loosening the ropes. "The brambles are just too strong."

Benjamin looked up at
the sky helplessly.
"Now I really have
ruined Peter's surprise
party," he whispered.

He hugged himself closely.
**"Rabbits are brave.
Rabbits are
brave."**

But, as he did so, he felt
the balloons in his pocket,
and suddenly he had a
BRILLIANT IDEA . . .

While Mr Tod was distracted, Benjamin whispered his plan in Lily's ear, then started blowing up an **ENORMOUS BALLOON.**

"What's the plan, Benjamin?" whispered Peter.

"Let's just say it's a surprise," said Lily, tying a paper chain round Mr Tod's feet.

Peter was confused but excited. There was nothing he loved more than **SURPRISES!**

Mr Tod turned round just as Benjamin finished blowing up the balloon.

"Quick! Hold on to me!" puffed Benjamin. Peter and Lily grabbed on tightly.

"IT'S WORKING! IT'S WORKING!" cried Peter.

The balloon gently floated towards the opening in the trap.

The dastardly fox desperately tried to grab the rabbits, but fell flat on his face!

"Drat! Outfoxed by rabbits! I'll get you next time!" he sneered.

The three rabbits floated **higher and higher** over the woods.

"Quick! Let out some air,"

cried Lily.

"We might just make it on time . . ."

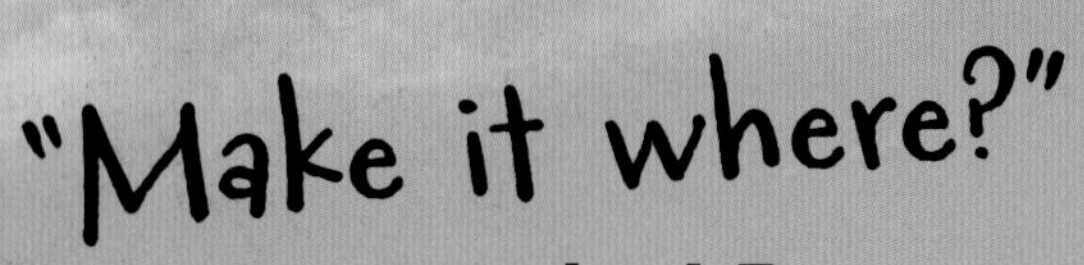

"Make it where?"

asked Peter.

"There!" said Benjamin, pointing down to the party in the next clearing.

But, as he pointed, he let out too much air and the three friends zoomed down to the ground, towards . . .

"A giant cake!" cheered Peter, as the three bunnies landed **SPLAT** right in the middle of it!

"Your giant cake," said Peter's mum, smiling. "SURPRISE!"

"At least it was a soft landing!" Benjamin giggled.

"Happy birthday, Peter!"

cheered all of Peter's family and friends.

Peter was delighted – he loved surprises. "I thought you'd all forgotten," he said, licking the delicious icing off his paws.

Everyone had a wonderful time at the party. There were plenty of games and tasty treats. They laughed and played until the sun went down.

"Sorry for getting us trapped, Peter," whispered Benjamin.

"What do you mean, sorry? I've had an adventure, cake and a surprise party!" replied Peter.

"It's been the best birthday **ever!**"